Perfectly Princess

Written by Lisa Thompson
Pictures by Andy and Inga Hamilton

Princess Daisy Boo was growing fast.

She had grown too tall for her ball gown.

Her feet were now too big for her shoes.

Her tiara was now too small for her head.

3

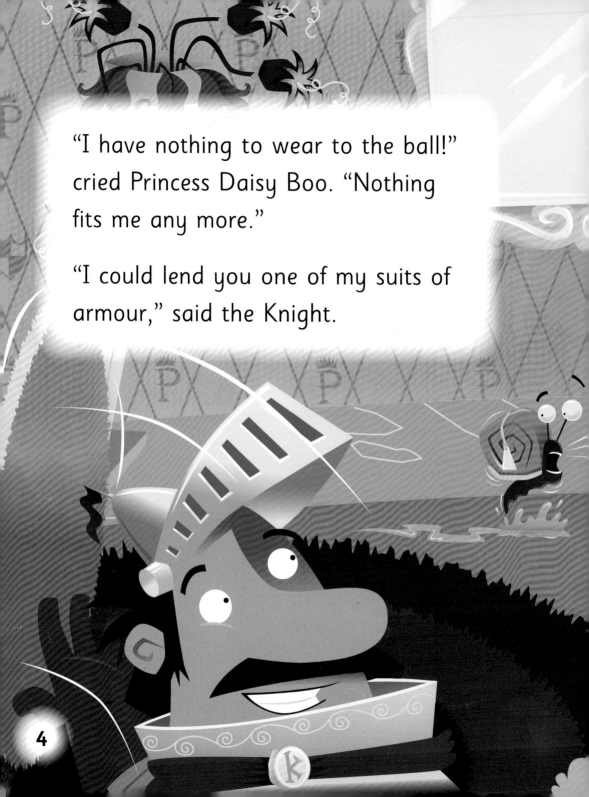

"I have nothing to wear to the ball!" cried Princess Daisy Boo. "Nothing fits me any more."

"I could lend you one of my suits of armour," said the Knight.

4

5

The Princess tried on the Knight's suit of armour.

"I don't think this suits me," she said.

"You can wear one of my dresses," said the Queen.

The Princess looked through the Queen's wardrobe. There were hundreds of dresses.

"I don't think anything here will look good on me," she said.

9

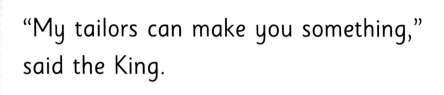

"My tailors can make you something," said the King.

He ordered his tailors to make something for the Princess to wear.

The Princess frowned. "It's not my style."

10

CATALOGUE

NEW
XXXXL
SIZES

11

Prince Axel tried to find something for the Princess to wear.

She was not at all happy with his bright idea.

"It's hopeless," said the Princess. "I won't be able to go to the ball."

There was a knock from inside her wardrobe.

"Let me out!" said a loud voice.

A very large fairy flew out of the wardrobe.

"Who are you?" asked the Princess.

"I am the Fairy Godmother of Wardrobes," said the Fairy. "I hear you are looking for a ball gown."

"With shoes and a tiara," said the Princess.

The Fairy Godmother of Wardrobes waved her wand.

The Princess was dressed from head to toe in flowers.

"This really does not suit me," said the Princess.

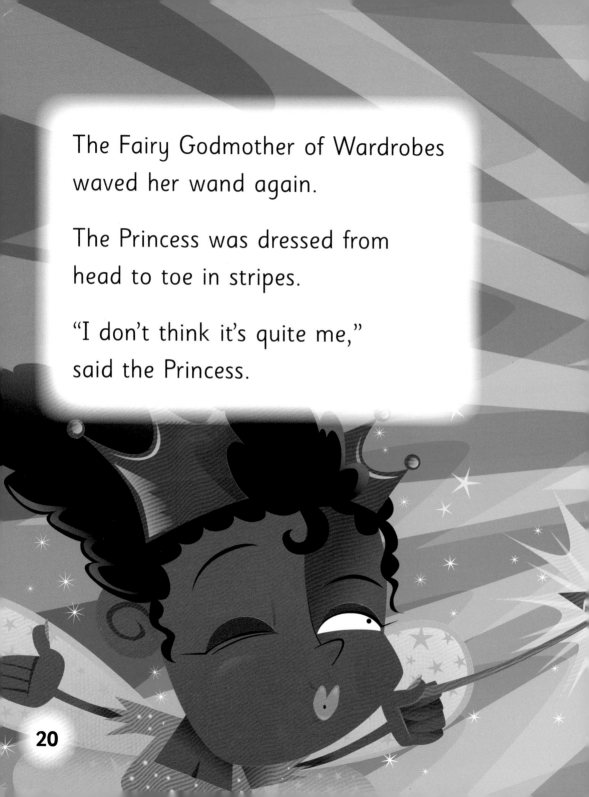

The Fairy Godmother of Wardrobes waved her wand again.

The Princess was dressed from head to toe in stripes.

"I don't think it's quite me," said the Princess.

The Fairy Godmother of Wardrobes waved her wand again.

This time the Princess was dressed from head to toe in pinks and purples.

"My favourite colours!" said the Princess. "This is very me. I am Pink and Purple Princess Perfect!"